Baby Bear's Christmas Kiss

RED FOX

UK | USA | Canada | Ireland | Australia | India | New Zealand | South Africa

Red Fox is part of the Penguin Random House group of companies
whose addresses can be found at global.penguinrandomhouse.com.

www.penguin.co.uk   www.puffin.co.uk   www.ladybird.co.uk

Penguin
Random House
UK

First published in Great Britain by The Bodley Head,
an imprint of Random House Children's Books
The Bodley Head edition published 2004
Red Fox edition published 2005
This edition published 2018
001

Copyright © John Prater, 2004

Printed in China
A CIP catalogue record for this book is available from the British Library

ISBN: 978–1–782–95884–0

All correspondence to:
Red Fox, Penguin Random House Children's
80 Strand, London WC2R 0RL

Baby Bear's Christmas Kiss

JOHN PRATER

RED FOX

It was Christmas Day!
The whole family were visiting Baby Bear and
Grandbear. That's Granny Bear, Uncle Bear,
Auntie Bear and four Cousin Bears.
The grown-ups warmed up by the fire,
while the little ones put their presents
under the tree. But they didn't seem
to be able to leave them alone.

Every present was shaken . . .

. . . prodded

. . . and sniffed.

Grandbear had an idea.
"You can open just one
present each, now!"

All the cousins ripped open their presents.

"Wow!" said Baby Bear. "What is it?"
"It's a toboggan," said Grandbear.
"What's a 'boggan?"
asked Baby Bear.
"I'll show you,"
said Uncle Bear.
"Come outside with me."

"Up the hill
we go!"
said Uncle Bear.

"Now watch closely,"
said Uncle Bear.
"First, you . . ."

"Hey!" cried Uncle Bear. "Wait! . . ."

Faster and *faster*
went Uncle Bear . . .

. . . until he met up with a snowbear!

"That was really funny," said Baby Bear.
"Can we have a go, now?"

Up the hill
they went again . . .

. . . and down

they came!

Again and again until Uncle Bear said . . .

"Oooh, I can smell yummy cooking.
It's time to go inside."

Grandbear met them at the door.
"Hello, snowbears! You're just
in time for Christmas dinner."

What a feast!

After dinner, the grown-ups were so
full they could hardly move.
The little ones played hide-and-seek.

It didn't take Baby Bear long to find Big Cousin Bear hiding under the tree. "This is my present to Mum and Dad," said Big Cousin Bear. "What are you giving Grandbear?"

"I haven't got a present for Grandbear!" said Baby Bear. "Never mind," said Big Cousin Bear. "It's your turn to hide now!"

While the others covered their eyes, and counted to ten, Baby Bear crept out of the room, through the kitchen, and into the garden.

But Baby Bear wasn't hiding. Baby Bear was going to find a present for Grandbear.

Grandbear likes snow, thought Baby Bear.
And stars. Something glistened and caught
Baby Bear's eye . . .

Baby Bear looked closer.
"Snowberries!"
said Baby Bear.
"All twinkly like
the star on the
Christmas
tree!"

Baby Bear picked
some berries, then
started to make
something out
of snow.

When it was
finished,
Baby Bear
hurried
back inside.

"Found you!"
called Cousin Bear.
"Come on, we're opening
the presents now."

Everyone was very excited!

"Happy Christmas,
Grandbear!"
said Baby Bear.
"I brought you
a snowberry
snowbear!"

"Mistletoe!" said
Grandbear. "That
deserves a special
Christmas kiss!
I'll put your lovely
present somewhere
where it won't melt."

All the grown-ups asked

if they could have a

Christmas kiss too.

The little ones weren't too sure, though.